The Fantastic Dragon Catcher

Charlie Bacon

The Fantastic
Dragon Catcher

by Gary Hogg

ILLUSTRATED BY ELISE SUMMERS

Little Buckaroo Books

Text copyright © 2016 by Gary Hogg
Illustrations copyright © by Elise Summers
Designed by Matt Shay
ISBN 978-0-93077-142-3

Printed in the U.S.A.

10 9 8 7 6 5 4 3 2 1

For Leslie Stitt,

One of the most intelligent, generous,

and insightful people I know.

Thanks for always being willing to share.

Contents

Chapter 1
The Horrible Creature

Charlie Bacon pounded on the bathroom door and yelled, "Grandpa, the dragon has escaped and it's chasing Grandma around the yard!"

"Good grief!" bellowed Grandpa. The door flew open and Grandpa blasted out of the room. "Come on," he shouted as he ran down the hall. "She's a killer!"

"The dragon's a killer?" asked Charlie as he chased after Grandpa.

"No, your grandma is!" shouted Grandpa as he dashed out the back door.

As soon as they got outside, they heard the

commotion. Grandma held a broom and was dueling with the dragon. Grandpa stepped between the two just as Grandma swung the broom. It smacked him on the side of the head. Just then the dragon jumped and bit him hard on the behind.

"Catch that dragon!" he shouted, looking at Charlie.

Charlie sprinted into the garage and came out with Grandpa's biggest fishing net. Grandma moved to her left to take another swipe at the dragon. With a loud squawk, the dragon flapped its wings and flew straight at her. Like a big league slugger, Grandma reared back to swing with all her might. She was going to send this dragon to outer space.

With a swoop of the net, Charlie bagged the dragon. At the same time, Grandpa snatched the broom out of Grandma's hands. Charlie hurried over

to the cage and shoved the dragon inside. He slammed the door and raced back to his grandparents.

Grandma was furious. "I will not have that horrible creature on our property for one more minute!" she yelled.

"But, Martha, that dragon is going to make us famous," said Grandpa.

"Stop calling that thing a dragon. It's a chicken," insisted Grandma.

"A dragon chicken from Vietnam," explained Grandpa. "They are very rare."

"Rare," scoffed Grandma. "It's going to be well done if it comes after me one more time. I'll fry that thing for dinner." She turned and marched into the house.

Grandpa hurried over to the dragon's cage. "How did she escape?" he asked.

"I don't know. One minute the door was latched

and the next thing I knew she was chasing Grandma," said Charlie. "She is one fast chicken."

"That's why I paid big bucks for her," said Grandpa. "With her long legs she's a shoo-in to win first place at the Super Cooper chicken race at the fair."

"Why can't she be in the chicken coop with the other hens?" asked Charlie.

"I'm feeding her a special mix of grains and vitamins to keep her in top running shape," replied Grandpa.

An old Ford truck drove into the driveway. "Oh no," said Grandpa. "It's Blanche Trudeau. Quick, cover the cage with that tarp. I don't want her to get a glimpse of the dragon."

"Why not?" asked Charlie.

"She's our main competition. There's no telling what she would do to keep our bird off the racetrack," said Grandpa.

Charlie quickly pulled a dirty brown tarp over the top of the cage as Blanche hopped out of her truck.

"Howdy, Milton," said the stout lady. An old straw hat covered her short gray hair. "Whatcha got under the tarp?"

"Nothing interesting," fibbed Grandpa.

"You sure you're not hiding anything? Maybe a new chicken that I should get a look at? Mac at the feed store said you had a newfangled monster bird imported for this year's race. He called it a dragon chicken," said Blanche.

Grandpa laughed and said, "Mac has no idea what he's talking about. I'm racing old Cluck Cluck."

Blanche strolled over to the fenced chicken run that was attached to the coop and asked, "Which one is Cluck Cluck?"

Grandpa whispered to Charlie, "Guard the dragon. And whatever you do, don't let Blanche look under that tarp. I'll get rid of her as fast as I can."

"Right," said Charlie. He watched as Grandpa entered the chicken run and came out carrying a rust-colored chicken.

Blanche squinted as she looked into Cluck Cluck's beady eyes. "She doesn't look all that fast," she said.

"Don't let those sweet eyes fool you. Cluck Cluck is as fast as greased lightning," said Grandpa.

While Grandpa returned Cluck Cluck to the coop, Blanche walked over to Charlie. "Is this your grandson?" she asked.

"That's Charlie. He's staying with us all week," said Grandpa.

"Nice to meet you, Charlie," said Blanche, shaking Charlie's hand. "Do you like fudge?"

"Oh yeah," said Charlie, licking his lips.

"Well, there's a fresh batch in the front seat of my truck. Why don't you go get you and your grandpa each a piece," said Blanche.

"Charlie's allergic to fudge," said Grandpa.

"No, I'm not," argued Charlie abandoning his post and hurrying over to the Ford. As soon as he was at the truck, Blanche picked up the corner of the tarp.

"Get away from there," ordered Grandpa.

"Just going to have a little look-see," said Blanche.

"There's nothing under there," stammered Grandpa.

"Then you won't mind if I do this," said Blanche, grinning. With a hard yank she jerked the tarp off the cage.

Hurrying back from the truck, Charlie nearly choked on his first bite of fudge. The cage was empty.

Chapter 2

A
Feather-Covered
Bowling Ball

The back door opened and out stepped Grandma. "Hi, Blanche, I thought I heard your voice. It's good to see you."

"Likewise," said Blanche. "Would you like a piece of fudge?"

Grandma's face bloomed into a smile. "If it's your famous homemade triple chocolate fudge, I do."

Leaving the door open, Grandma headed straight for the Ford truck to meet Blanche. While the ladies chatted, Grandpa hurried over to Charlie. "Where did the dragon go?" he whispered.

"I don't know," answered Charlie. "But as soon

as she spots Grandma, there's going to be another chicken war."

Grandpa's eyes popped open wide as he spotted the dragon chicken strut through the open door and into the house. "She's in the house," he said softly.

"No she's not. She's right there talking to Mrs. Trudeau," stated Charlie.

"The dragon is in the house," explained Grandpa. "I'll stall your grandmother. You go get that chicken before it makes a mess of things."

"You can count on me," Charlie said as he sprinted toward the house.

"What's your hurry?" asked Grandma.

"Bathroom emergency," shouted Charlie as he zoomed through the back door. He hurried into the living room and did a fast search. There was no sign of the dragon.

Next he dashed into the bathroom and looked in the tub and behind the toilet. The dragon was not there. Charlie zipped into the kitchen. He spotted two freshly baked pies cooling on the windowsill but the dragon was nowhere in sight.

Charlie heard voices and turned to see Grandma and Blanche standing in the doorway. "Don't touch those apple pies," said Grandma. "They're for the pie baking contest at the fair."

Blanche inspected the perfectly baked pies. "Martha, you are a fabulous baker. I don't know how you do it."

"Baking is how I relieve my stress," admitted Grandma.

Grandpa shuffled into the room and Blanche said, "Being married to Milton must keep you baking all the time."

Both ladies laughed while Grandpa pulled Charlie into the next room.

"Did you find the dragon?" asked Grandpa.

"No," said Charlie. "I don't think she's in the house."

At that moment they heard a loud clucking sound coming from Grandpa and Grandma's bedroom. "Go get her. And don't let her touch any of Grandma's stuff," insisted Grandpa as he headed back into the kitchen.

Charlie found the dragon sitting on top of his grandparents' bed. She was getting comfortable on Grandma's favorite pillow. Charlie inched over to the bed, being careful not to startle the bird.

"Now I've got you," said Charlie as he lunged at the chicken. His arms came up empty as the dragon hopped off the pillow and landed on top of Grandma's nightstand. Charlie took another grab at the chicken.

He missed again but managed to tip over the lamp and knock Grandma's jewelry box to the floor.

The chicken flapped its wings and jumped on top of the dresser drawers. Like a feather-covered bowling ball, the chicken rolled through Grandma's favorite pictures of her grandchildren. The picture frames tumbled like pins in a bowling alley.

With Charlie hot on its tail, the dragon flew into the closet. Charlie tore through his grandparents' clothes like a tornado. The dragon zipped between his legs and headed out the bedroom door.

Charlie staggered out of the closet with Grandma's favorite floral pink nightgown wrapped around his right leg. He made a beeline for the escaping bird and blasted into the living room.

The dragon took a quick right turn and charged into the kitchen. Grandma and Blanche were

screaming like maniacs when Charlie stumbled into the room dragging the nightgown.

"I've got her," shouted Grandpa. He reached for the wild chicken and fell to the floor as the bird squirted through his hands.

The dragon spotted the open window and made a jump for it. Grandma yelled, "Oh no, not my pies!" With a flying leap, Charlie hurdled over Grandpa and swopped up a pie in each hand just as the chicken flew out the window.

"I saved them," shouted Charlie. He took a step forward and tripped on Grandma's nightgown. He staggered and fell to the floor next to Grandpa. Both apple pies flew in the air and landed on top of Charlie and Grandpa's heads. Chunks of sweet apples slid down their faces and dripped onto the floor.

Blanche quickly stepped over to the window to get

a glimpse of the dragon chicken as it charged across the yard. "I just remembered I need to get home," she said hurrying out the door.

Grandma's face flushed hot red. She stared daggers at Charlie and Grandpa.

"I can explain," said Grandpa.

"No, I will explain," interrupted Grandma. "You two chicken racers will clean up this mess and whatever other messes this foul fowl has created. I'm going to the store to get some apples and ingredients to bake some new pies. When I get back you will assist me in baking those pies. Am I being clear?"

"Perfectly clear," said Grandpa, digging pie crust out of his ears.

Charlie jumped up when he heard Blanche's truck tires squeal. He looked out the window and yelled, "Blanche Trudeau is stealing the dragon!"

Chapter 3
Cock-a-doodle-do

"Good grief!" hollered Grandpa. He slipped in the pie filling as he struggled to his feet. By the time he made it out the back door, Blanche's truck was racing down the road.

"That two-bit chicken thief!" he shouted, kicking the dirt. "She will not get away with this."

"Blanche is not a chicken thief," insisted Grandma.

"I saw the dragon in the back of her truck," declared Charlie.

"I'm calling the police," said Grandpa.

"Not so quick," said Grandma. She went into the house and returned with her purse. "I'll swing by

Blanche's place on my way back from the store and clear this whole thing up. While I'm gone you two should have enough time to clean up this mess. I don't want to see as much as a feather in my house when I return."

She slid behind the steering wheel of Grandpa's truck and headed down the road. Grandpa and Charlie spent the next hour cleaning the house. They were just finishing when Grandma returned.

"You were right," said Grandma. "The dragon was in the back of Blanche's truck. But she swears she didn't put it there and I believe her."

"Maybe the dragon was trying to run away," suggested Charlie. "She likes to escape. I better go put her in her cage before she takes off again."

Charlie raced outside, but ran right back into the house. "There's a weird-looking white chicken in the back of the truck with the dragon!" he exclaimed.

"That's Zippy," said Grandma. "I bought her from Blanche. I'm going to enter her in the chicken race."

"You're what?" blurted Grandpa.

"I'm entering Zippy in the Super Cooper chicken race," said Grandma. "She's very fast."

Grandpa rubbed his forehead like he just got a huge headache. "Did Blanche talk you into this?" he asked.

"Absolutely not," said Grandma. "It was my idea. You never mentioned the winner of the Super Cooper race gets two hundred dollars."

"Two hundred dollars!" gasped Charlie. "That's a lot of chicken feed. Can kids enter?"

Grandpa laughed and said, "No, you have to be a chicken."

"No, I mean can a kid enter a chicken in the race?" asked Charlie.

"I don't know why not," said Grandpa.

Charlie rubbed his hands together as he thought about the prize money. "I want to enter Cluck Cluck. You told Mrs. Trudeau that she was as fast as greased lightning."

"I was exaggerating," said Grandpa. "Cluck Cluck is the laziest critter on the place."

"I'll motivate her," said Charlie.

"There's a twenty-five dollar entry fee," said Grandpa. "Do you have that kind of money?"

"No, but I can earn it," offered Charlie. "I'm a hard worker."

"The race is in two days. That doesn't give you much time," said Grandpa.

"If I get the money, can I enter Cluck Cluck in the Super Cooper race?" asked Charlie.

While Grandpa was thinking it over, Grandma

said, "Of course you can."

"Cock-a-doodle-do!" crowed Charlie, racing out the door. "I'm going to be rich."

Grandpa and Grandma followed Charlie outside. Grandpa looked at Grandma's new chicken, Zippy. "She's a silkie. They are the weirdest-looking chickens on the planet," he said.

"She's prettier than that monster chicken of yours," said Grandma.

The dragon chicken let out a loud squawk and flapped her wings. Grandpa lifted the dragon out of the back of the truck and placed her in the cage.

"Keep that monster away from me," said Grandma.

"Don't worry," said Grandpa. "I'm going to lock the cage. She will not be escaping again."

Charlie opened the chicken coop's door while Grandma placed her new chicken inside with the

Rhode Island Reds. Zippy clucked and strutted in a circle.

"She's doing the chicken dance," said Charlie, laughing. He flapped his arms and copied Zippy's moves.

"She's trying to see what the pecking order is," explained Grandpa. "There's always one chicken that's the boss."

"What's the pecking order with you and Grandma?" asked Charlie.

Grandpa let out a loud laugh and said, "Everyone knows who the big chicken is in our house."

"Yes, Milton, you are the big chicken," said Grandma with a grin. "Now come along. We have pies to bake."

"Yes, dear," said the big chicken as he followed Grandma back into the house.

Chapter 4

Elbow Grease

Grandpa was already wearing one of Grandma's aprons by the time Charlie reported for pie-making duty. Charlie washed his hands and put on a bright blue apron.

Grandma mixed the dough for the crusts while Charlie and Grandpa peeled and sliced the apples. After they placed them in a large mixing bowl, Grandma added two cups of sugar, a pinch of salt, a dash of nutmeg, a scoop of cinnamon, a little flour, and a squeeze of lemon juice.

"And now for the secret ingredient," said Grandma. "Every winner has a secret ingredient."

"What's the secret ingredient?" asked Charlie.

"If I told you, it wouldn't be a secret," said Grandma, smiling. "Close your eyes. You too Milton."

"This is ridiculous," grumbled Grandpa. Grandma put her hands on her hips and he quickly shut his eyes.

After a moment, Grandma said, "You can open your eyes now." She then poured the pie filling into the two pie crusts she had prepared. She placed the top crusts on the pies and popped them into the oven.

After supper, Grandma sliced one of the freshly baked pies. She lifted out three large slices and topped them with scoops of vanilla ice cream.

Charlie shoved a forkful of pie into his mouth. "This is the best pie in the universe," he said between chews.

"It sure is," agreed Grandpa, licking his lips.

Grandma finished her slice of pie and said,

"Charlie, I'll pay you two dollars to wash the dishes tonight. You just need to make twenty-three more dollars and you'll have enough to enter Cluck Cluck in the Super Cooper race."

"You got it," said Charlie. As soon as the last dish was dried, he headed for the door.

"Where are you going?" asked Grandma.

"To make twenty-three dollars," answered Charlie. "I'm sure some of your neighbors would pay to have their dishes professionally washed."

"I'll pay you two dollars to wash my truck," offered Grandpa.

"Ten dollars," said Charlie. "Trucks are a lot bigger than bowls and plates."

"Five dollars," countered Grandpa.

"Eight bucks and you got a deal," said Charlie.

"Deal," said Grandpa. "Use lots of elbow grease; I

31

want that baby to shine."

"Oh, it'll shine," said Charlie. "I'll use so much grease you won't recognize it when I'm done."

"That a boy," said Grandpa. "You'll find everything you need in the garage."

Charlie hustled into the garage to get the supplies. First, he dragged the step ladder out to the driveway. Next he took out a pile of rags and placed them on the ladder.

"Now, where does Grandpa keep the elbow grease?" said Charlie to himself. He found a half-filled can of paint, a jug of oil, and a plastic bottle of weed killer, but no elbow grease. He was about to give up and go ask Grandpa for help when he spotted a gallon can of axle grease.

"Bingo," said Charlie. "I'll bet Grandpa meant axle grease instead of elbow grease." He lugged the can out

to Grandpa's truck, pried off the lid, and went right to work.

Charlie scooped up a glob of the smoky gray grease with one of the rags and began rubbing it on the truck. The grease left a thick, dirty film on the red truck. By the time the truck was covered in grease, Charlie was too.

He stood back and examined the truck. "Grandpa was right. It takes lots of grease to get a truck clean. I need some more," said Charlie.

When he couldn't find another can of grease in the garage, he decided to ask Grandpa. Charlie went to the back door and tried to turn the doorknob. His hands were so slippery, he couldn't get a grip. He knocked hard on the door.

As soon as Grandpa opened the door, Charlie blurted out, "I need more grease. I've covered the whole truck and it still looks dirty."

Grandpa gasped, "What on earth are you doing?"

"You said to use lots of elbow grease. I couldn't find elbow grease so I used axle grease," said Charlie, beaming. "You were right. It takes a lot to get a truck clean."

"Elbow grease is not actual grease. It's a phrase that means hard work," said Grandpa. His voice got louder with every word.

"Well, I used grease and hard work," said Charlie proudly.

Grandpa marched out the door and into the driveway to look at his truck. His face turned bright red. At that moment, a strong wind began to blow. Leaves and dust swirled in the air and stuck to the grease-covered truck.

"Good grief, it's a sticky mess!" shouted Grandpa.

Grandma heard Grandpa's angry voice and came out of the house. "Milton, what has got you so upset?" she asked. Grandpa was speechless as he pointed at the truck.

"Oh dear," said Grandma. "What happened?"

"I used the wrong kind of grease," explained Charlie. "Grandpa said use elbow grease, but I used axle grease."

Grandma began to laugh. The more the wind blew, the harder she laughed. Grandpa glared at her but she laughed anyway. She laughed so hard, tears formed in her eyes.

"This is not funny," insisted Grandpa.

"I know," said Grandma, shaking her head. "It's hilarious."

Grandpa climbed in the truck and started the engine. He turned on the windshield wipers and grease smeared back and forth across the windshield. That made Grandma laugh even harder.

"I'm going to the carwash and try to fix this mess," said Grandpa.

"What about my eight dollars?" asked Charlie. Grandpa didn't answer. He revved the engine and headed for town.

Chapter 5
That Dumb Bird

Charlie took off his greasy clothes and headed straight to the shower. He scrubbed with hot water until most of the grease was gone. He was wearing his favorite pajamas when Grandpa returned home.

"Did you get the grease off the truck?" asked Grandma.

"I had to run it through the carwash three times but I finally got it clean as a whistle," said Grandpa. He reached into his wallet and gave Charlie eight dollars.

"But I didn't clean the truck," said Charlie. "I made it messier."

"A deal's a deal," said Grandpa. "I should have given

you better directions. You didn't know what elbow grease was."

"I do now," said Charlie, taking the money. "Tomorrow I'm going to use elbow grease to make fifteen more dollars."

After playing two games of checkers with Grandpa, Charlie headed to bed. When he woke up the next morning, Grandpa was already outside training the dragon. He had built a long oval racetrack out of chicken wire. The dragon stood at one end with her beak poking through the wire.

"Turn around and run, you birdbrain!" yelled Grandpa.

The huge chicken paid no attention. Grandpa ran around the outside of the track waving his arms. That did the trick. The dragon spun around and got up a good head of steam before flapping its wings and flying over the chicken-wire fence.

"There she goes again," said Charlie as the dragon raced toward the house.

"That dumb bird is going to be the death of me," shouted Grandpa as he took after the large chicken.

Charlie ran into the garage and came out with the fishing net. He chased after the dragon like an Olympic runner.

"Got her!" he yelled as he dropped the net over the crazy bird.

Grandpa was bent over gasping for air when Grandma opened the kitchen window and called out, "Breakfast is ready."

Charlie handed the chicken to Grandpa and raced into the house. The smell of bacon and eggs filled the air.

"Wash up," said Grandma.

Charlie did a U-turn and hurried into the bathroom. He washed his hands and sped back to the kitchen. Grandma scooped some scrambled eggs onto a plate and placed four strips of crispy bacon next to them. She topped off the breakfast with a buttered slice of her homemade bread and a glass of milk.

"Grandma, you're the best," said Charlie, biting into a slice of bacon. Grandpa was still breathing hard when he made it into the kitchen.

"How did the training session go?" asked Grandma.

"I'm still working out the kinks," said Grandpa, holding his sore back.

"I don't know who has more kinks, you or that bird," said Grandma.

She placed a plate of food in front of Grandpa. "You boys are on your own this morning. I need to drop my apple pie off at the fair."

"You've got the blue ribbon in the bag," said Charlie.

"We'll find out tomorrow if you're right," said Grandma as she placed the apple pie in a round straw basket.

"I'll do the dishes," offered Charlie. "Do you still pay two dollars?"

"I'll give you five dollars to wash the dishes, feed the chickens, and gather the eggs," said Grandma.

Charlie was filling the sink with water when Grandma left for the fair. He washed and dried the frying pan and breakfast dishes. After putting them back in the cupboard he headed out to gather the eggs. As soon as he stepped into the backyard, the dragon rushed past him.

"Catch that chicken!" yelled Grandpa.

Charlie grabbed the fishing net and hid behind the

maple tree. It wasn't long before the dragon sprinted past. Charlie scooped up the dashing chicken with a quick swish of the net.

"What if she gets loose at the fair tomorrow?" asked Charlie.

"That would be a disaster," said Grandpa. "Let's hope it doesn't happen."

Charlie filled the chicken feeder and water dish. He then gathered five large brown eggs from the nests. When he turned to leave, Cluck Cluck was right behind him. Charlie set the eggs down and picked up the hen. He petted her soft feathers before placing her on one of the nests.

"You better get some rest because we've got a big afternoon," said Charlie. "But first I have to earn ten more dollars."

Chapter 6

Working Man

Charlie got Grandma's lavender colored cruiser bike off the back porch and filled the basket with cleaning supplies. He pedaled down the road to Mr. Richardson's house. He knocked on the front door. When Mr. Richardson opened the door, Charlie was holding a scrub brush.

"Can I help you?" asked Mr. Richardson.

"No, but I can help you," said Charlie. "I'm Charlie Bacon and I'll wash your dishes for two dollars."

"No, thank you," said Mr. Richardson as he closed the door.

Charlie put the scrub brush back in the basket and

picked up a window washing squeegee. He knocked on the door a second time.

Mr. Richardson opened the door and said, "Now what?"

"I'll wash your windows for five dollars," offered Charlie.

"Nope," said Mr. Richardson, closing the door again.

Charlie put the squeegee back in the basket and picked up a shoeshine rag. He knocked again. When Mr. Richardson opened the door, Charlie said, "Shoeshine for a buck."

"I wear sneakers," said Mr. Richardson. Before he could shut the door, Charlie blurted, "Car wash? I'll use extra elbow grease."

"You are a very persistent boy," said Mr. Richardson. "How about I give you a dollar to leave me alone?"

"Deal," said Charlie, holding out his hand.

He rode Grandma's bike to the next house on the street. Darlene Wells answered the door. "Do you need any chores done? I work cheap," said Charlie with a huge grin.

"How much do you charge to scoop poop?" asked Mrs. Wells. Just then a puny Pomeranian whisked through her legs.

Charlie sized up the petite dog and said, "Three dollars."

"Good," said Mrs. Wells. "Barney has made a disaster of the backyard."

"Is this Barney?" asked Charlie.

Mrs. Wells laughed and said, "Heavens no, this is Princess."

That's when a pony-sized Great Dane charged

around the side of the house. "That knucklehead is Barney."

"Oh no," groaned Charlie. It took him almost an hour to clean all of Barney's jumbo-sized doggie doodies. Darlene paid him the three dollars and chipped in a dollar tip.

Before riding to the next house, Charlie stopped to count his money. He needed five more dollars. He pedaled down the street and stopped in the driveway of a sky-blue house.

Charlie decided to check out the backyard before he agreed to any more poop-scooping jobs. He circled around behind the house and froze in place. There was an old Ford truck parked in the backyard. This was Blanche Trudeau's home.

The theme music from the movie Rocky was blaring from behind a huge chicken coop at the back of the property. Charlie's curiosity got the best of him. He sneaked over to the chicken coop and slowly inched his way along the wall until he could get a glimpse behind the building.

Blanche was wearing a bright yellow tracksuit with a coach's whistle around her neck. When the music stopped, Charlie could hear Blanche's high-pitched voice giving a pep talk to a tall, white chicken.

"You are a champion! You are a winner! You are invincible!" shouted Blanche.

She placed the whistle in her mouth and held up a stopwatch in her left hand. She moved her thumb over the start button on the stopwatch and pressed it down at the exact moment she blew the whistle.

Tiny puffs of dust flew in the air as the chicken raced down the track. When it looked like the bird was running at top speed, Blanche gave another mighty

blast on the whistle. The shrill sound of the whistle ignited something in the bird that propelled it even faster down the track.

Charlie was amazed. He had never seen a chicken move that fast. When the bird reached the finish line, Blanche clicked the stopwatch and looked at the time.

"That's my baby!" she shouted. "That sneaky Milton and his super bird don't stand a chance against you."

Charlie had seen enough. But when he turned to leave, he stepped on the end of a rake that was lying in the grass. The rake flipped up and the handle smacked him hard on the forehead.

"Ow!" blurted out Charlie. He immediately covered his mouth with his right hand and held his breath. Maybe Mrs. Trudeau hadn't heard him. He began to tippy-toe along the side of the coop. When he turned the corner, he was face-to-face with Blanche Trudeau.

Chapter 7

All's Fair in Love and Chicken Racing

"Charlie Bacon, what are you doing sneaking around my chicken coop?" asked Blanche. "Did your grandpa send you to spy on me?"

"I'm not a spy," explained Charlie. "I was in your yard and heard the loud music."

"What were you doing in my yard?" asked Blanche.

"I'm looking for work," said Charlie. "I need to make five more dollars so I can enter Cluck Cluck in the Super Cooper race tomorrow."

Blanche rubbed her chin with her left hand as she thought. "What do you know about chicken racing?" she asked.

"I know the winner gets two hundred bucks," said Charlie.

Blanche let out a loud laugh and said, "I like you, Charlie Bacon. Have you ever cleaned a chicken coop before?"

"It doesn't sound very fun," said Charlie.

"It's not, but I'll pay you five dollars if you do a good job," said Blanche.

"Oh, I'll do a great job," said Charlie.

Blanche stepped into the house and returned with a bowl of strawberries. "Open the gate to the chicken run," she called out.

Charlie opened the gate and Blanche yelled, "STRAWBERRIES!"

The word "strawberries" had some kind of magical effect on the birds. They seemed to transform from chickens into cheetahs right before Charlie's eyes. The charging hens raced to Blanche.

"Watch this," said Blanche. She took a strawberry and launched it in the air. Like a team of miniature football players the chickens charged after the berry. A snowy white chicken blasted past the rest of the birds and without breaking stride jumped in the air and snagged the red berry.

"That's Twinkle Toes," said Blanche. "She's my superstar."

Next Blanche placed a strawberry on top of Charlie's head. "Don't move," she instructed.

Charlie stood as still as a statue while a little hen ran toward him. She flapped her wings twice before landing on top of his head. The hen pecked the strawberry and hopped back to the ground.

"She's amazing," said Charlie.

"You haven't seen anything yet," said Blanche. She

picked up a pudgy-looking hen and placed her on the bank of a small pond. She then tossed a strawberry into the water.

The chicken plunged headfirst into the pond, swam over to the strawberry, and plucked it out of the water. She swam to the other side with the strawberry in her beak. When she was back on land, she devoured the juicy fruit.

"I didn't know chickens could swim," Charlie said in awe.

"Chickens can do almost anything when they are properly motivated," said Blanche.

"Can they scrub the toilet?" asked Charlie.

"No," said Blanche.

"Can they fight a shark?" asked Charlie.

"Are you going to stand here and be ridiculous or are you going to clean the chicken coop?" said

Blanche.

Charlie grabbed a shovel and scooped all the chicken droppings into a wheelbarrow. Next, he took the hose and gave Blanche's coop a good washing. Finally, he emptied the straw out of the nests and replaced it with fresh bedding.

"All done," called out Charlie.

Like the leader of a marching band, Blanche led the birds back into the coop. "What do you think?" asked Charlie.

"It's not what I think, it's what Gerdy thinks," said Blanche. The plumpest hen of the brood hopped into one of the freshly made nests and wiggled her behind into the soft straw.

"You passed inspection. Gerdy likes it," said Blanche. "Come into the house and I'll pay you."

Charlie followed Blanche into the kitchen. There

was a basketful of ripe strawberries on the kitchen table

You can have all the strawberries you want," said Blanche. "I'll be right back with your money."

When Blanche left the room, Charlie quickly washed his hands and bit into a juicy strawberry. He thought about chickens cleaning a toilet and started to laugh. He was still giggling when Blanche came back into the kitchen.

"What's so funny?" she asked.

"I was just thinking about toilet-scrubbing chickens," confessed Charlie.

"You really are an odd boy," said Blanche as she handed him five single dollar bills. "Do yourself a favor and just keep the money. There's not a bird alive that can outrun my Twinkle Toes."

"What about Zippy?" asked Charlie. "Grandma

says you told her that Zippy was super fast."

Blanche flashed a mischievous smile and said, "Zippy is really fast. Too bad she's terrified of loud noises."

"The dragon isn't afraid of anything," said Charlie. "She might beat Twinkle Toes."

Blanche laughed, "That's why I brought her over here yesterday. It turns out that bird is a real nut job."

Charlie's eyes widened as he said, "I thought the dragon jumped in your truck without you knowing about it."

Blanche flashed her smile again and confessed, "I may have given her a little boost into the truck."

"That's cheating," said Charlie.

"All's fair in love and chicken racing," said Blanche.

Charlie picked up the basketful of strawberries and headed for the door.

"Where are you taking my strawberries?" asked Blanche.

"You said I could have all I wanted," said Charlie, flashing a mischievous smile of his own.

"You're taking them all?" asked Blanche.

Charlie stopped and said, "Of course not." He took a single strawberry out of the basket and placed it on the kitchen counter.

He was almost out of the door when he turned and said, "Thanks for the advice."

"What advice?" asked Blanche.

"All's fair in love and chicken racing," said Charlie, shutting the door behind him.

Chapter 8

Taking on the Dragon

After lunch Charlie took a handful of the strawberries and hurried outside. He took Cluck Cluck out of the chicken coop and set her down in the dirt behind Grandpa's house.

"Every winner needs a secret ingredient," explained Charlie. He held up a strawberry and in a loud voice said, "Strawberry." He then gave Cluck Cluck a juicy bit of the berry. The sweetness of the strawberry energized the chicken. She stretched and strutted around the yard.

Charlie repeated the process over and over until all he had to do was say the word and Cluck Cluck was scratching the dirt with excitement for the fruit.

"Now you need to know what going fast feels like," said Charlie.

He placed Cluck Cluck in the basket of Grandma's bike. Charlie pedaled slowly while the nervous hen peeked over the top of the basket. Soon she was comfortable enough to poke her whole head up and feel the breeze in her feathers.

The faster Charlie pedaled, the more Cluck Cluck loved it. When he was going full speed the hen hopped onto the handlebars and stuck her wings out. She was soaring and loving it.

Charlie slowly brought the bike to a stop and gave Cluck Cluck a juicy bite of strawberry. "You love strawberries and you love going fast," he said. "Now we just have to put the two of them together."

Charlie set Cluck Cluck on the driveway and

began pedaling back to Grandpa's house. He yelled "strawberry," and Cluck Cluck followed the bike. He pedaled harder and Cluck Cluck ran faster. When they got back to Grandpa's house, Charlie rewarded the hen with a strawberry.

After repeating the routine three more times, Charlie lifted the hen into his arms and petted her softly. Cluck Cluck rested her head on his arm. She had a new best friend.

Grandpa came out of the house and asked, "How's the training going?"

"Berry good," said Charlie.

"I hope Cluck Cluck likes dragon dust. She'll be eating plenty when she gets on the track with my bird," said Grandpa.

"Don't be so sure," said Charlie. "Cluck Cluck is pretty fast."

"Let's see just how fast she is," said Grandpa. "How about a little race?"

Charlie patted Cluck Cluck's head and whispered, "What about it, girl? Do you want to take on the dragon?"

Cluck Cluck wiggled and tried to get out of Charlie's arms. "I'll take that as a yes," said Charlie.

"This is going to be fun," said Grandpa as he got the dragon out of her cage.

"Should we invite Grandma and Zippy?" asked Charlie.

"The more the merrier," answered Grandpa.

The dragon was already on the oval track when Charlie and Grandma showed up with their birds. The huge chicken was scratching the dirt like a fighting bull.

"Let's get this race started," said Grandpa.

Grandma placed Zippy on the track. The exotic white chicken fluffed her feathers and pranced up and down the track. Charlie set Cluck Cluck on the dirt track and fed her a tiny piece of a strawberry.

"Let's line them up," said Grandpa. When the birds were all in a row he pulled a starter's pistol out of his pocket. When he fired it into the air, Zippy let out a loud squawk and fell over on the ground.

The dragon was off in a flash. With each step she gained speed. Cluck Cluck sprinted down the track just behind the dragon.

Charlie yelled "strawberry," and Cluck Cluck picked up the pace. She pulled even with the dragon. They were running neck and neck when the dragon suddenly veered to her right, slamming Cluck Cluck into the fence.

Cluck Cluck rolled three times before getting back

on her feet. She jumped up and began to run. She was now racing full speed the wrong way around the track.

"Turn around, Cluck Cluck!" yelled Charlie. "Turn around!"

The dragon dropped her head and headed straight for Cluck Cluck. They were on a head-on collision course. This was a real-life game of chicken, and feathers were about to fly.

In the split second before the two chickens crashed, Cluck Cluck jumped high in the air and the dragon charged right under her.

"Wow!" yelled Charlie. "Did you see that? Cluck Cluck is a Superbird."

"Super dumb bird," said Grandpa. "She almost killed my chicken." He picked up the dragon and returned her to the cage.

Grandma decided not to enter Zippy in the Super

Cooper. "The poor dear has a nervous condition," said Grandma. "Blanche doesn't know about it or she wouldn't have sold her to me for the race."

"Mrs. Trudeau is a cheater," said Charlie. "When I was at her house this morning she told about Zippy's problem and confessed to taking the dragon. She said that all's fair in love and chicken racing."

"Well, she's wrong about that," said Grandma. "And someday she'll learn her lesson.

Chapter 9

Wild Bull Rider

The next morning Grandpa came out of his bedroom wearing his cowboy hat. "Let's go to the fair," he said, heading for the door.

Grandpa and Charlie got two small wire cages out of the garage and put them in the back of the truck. They placed Cluck Cluck and the dragon in the cages and closed the doors.

Grandpa looped a plastic zip tie around the latch of the dragon's cage. With a quick tug, he zipped it tight.

"That will keep this Houdini of a hen in her cage," he said.

Charlie jumped into the back seat of the truck.

"Let's get this show on the road," he said, buckling his seatbelt.

The fairgrounds were hopping with excitement when they arrived. Charlie rolled down the window and stuck his head out to get a better look.

"This place is huge," he said. "Can we see it all?"

"First we have to drop our birds off in the poultry barn and sign up for the race," said Grandpa. He found a parking spot behind the livestock barns and they unloaded the cages.

Charlie looked at the long row of buildings. There was a different barn for each variety of farm animal.

"Cattle, swine, sheep, goats, horses, rabbits," said Charlie as he read the names on the barns. Finally he announced, "There's the poultry barn. Follow me."

The barn was full of all kinds of birds. Besides chickens, there were turkeys, ducks, geese, and even some peacocks. "Are all these birds going to be in the race?" asked Charlie.

"Heavens no," said Grandpa. "Most of these feathered beauties are here for the judged contests. The Super Cooper racers are in the back."

Grandma and Charlie followed Grandpa to the back of the building. There they saw Blanche Trudeau. She was wearing a flamingo pink T-shirt. It was customized with the words "Team Twinkle Toes — Born to Run."

"Where's Zippy?" asked Blanche.

"It turns out Zippy is afraid of loud noises," said Grandma. "You didn't mention it when I paid for her."

"It must have slipped my mind," said Blanche, flashing a sly smile.

Grandpa and Charlie placed the cages at the end of the row. When they walked over to the registration desk, Grandma left to see if her pie had won a ribbon.

"We'd like to sign up for the Super Cooper chicken race," said Grandpa.

"Easy peasy," said the lady in a sunshiny voice. "Fill out these forms. It'll be twenty-five dollars for each entry."

After they completed the forms and paid their entry money, Charlie and Grandpa went to have a look around. Charlie had fair fever. He couldn't wait to take in all of the activities.

"Can we ride the mechanical bull? Can we get some cotton candy? Can we enter the pickle-eating contest? Can we ride the Ferris Wheel?" he blurted out in rapid fire.

"Hold your horses," said Grandpa. "We can only do one thing at a time. Let's start with the mechanical bull and go from there."

There were three people in line ahead of Charlie and Grandpa at the mechanical bull. Charlie watched as the operator used a joystick to control the bull's speed.

"Have you ever ridden a bucking bull?" Charlie asked while they waited.

Grandpa chuckled and bragged, "There wasn't a bull that I couldn't ride in my younger days. I could've gone pro, but I wanted something more challenging."

"Is that why you became a plumber?" asked Charlie.

"I'll take a wild bull over a plugged toilet any day of the week," said Grandpa.

When it was their turn, Grandpa paid the operator for two rides on Tornado. Charlie climbed on first. He pulled his hat down tight and gritted his teeth. Tornado started slow with a few bucks and a couple of spins. When Charlie yelled, "Yee haw!" the operator turned up the heat. Charlie lasted three seconds before flying off and landing on the padded floor.

Grandpa was up next. While he was getting settled on top of Tornado, Charlie had a conversation with the operator.

"You don't have to hold back. There's never been a bull that could toss him," said Charlie.

The operator grinned and said, "Finally, I get someone who knows how to ride."

Grandpa put on a leather glove and crammed his hand into the handle. "Is it supposed to be this tight?" he asked.

"The tighter the better," answered the operator.

"But it's stuck," said Grandpa, trying to get his hand back out.

At that moment, the operator cranked the joystick

and Tornado sprang to life. The front of the bull dropped down low and then quickly jerked back up. Grandpa's eyes popped open wide as his hat flew off his head and landed on the floor.

"No! No!" yelled Grandpa.

"What did he say?" asked the operator.

"I think he said, 'Go! Go!'" said Charlie.

"Right on," said the operator, jerking the joystick back and forth. After several monster-sized bucks, the operator cranked the joystick to send Tornado into a death spin. Grandpa's legs slid off the bull and into the air. His body looked like a whirling helicopter blade as Tornado dipped and rotated, faster and faster.

The operator pulled hard on the joystick and Tornado reared forward and then crashed backward. That jerked Grandpa's hand free and he flew all the way across the padded floor, where he landed on top

of his cowboy hat.

Grandpa slowly stood up and pulled on his smashed hat. He staggered past Charlie and collapsed on a bench.

"Are you ready to eat some fried pickles?" asked Charlie.

Before Grandpa could answer, Grandma came rushing over.

"Did your pie win?" asked Charlie.

"Yes, but that's not important right now," gasped Grandma. "Milton, your chicken has disappeared!"

"Good grief," said Grandpa. "Help me up. We've got a dragon to catch."

Chapter 10
Pies in the Sky

They hurried back to the poultry barn and examined the dragon's cage. The zip tie was lying on the ground and the chicken was gone.

"Has anyone seen a runaway chicken?" yelled Grandpa.

"That crazy-looking bird took out of here like her feathers were on fire," answered a short, stocky man.

"Did you see how she got out of her cage?" asked Grandma.

"No, but Blanche Trudeau did," said the man. "She was standing next to the cage when your bird got loose."

"Where's Blanche now?" asked Grandma.

"She disappeared shortly after your chicken flew the coop," said the man.

Grandpa looked at his watch and said, "We don't have any time to waste. Let's find that bird."

After two hours the dragon was still on the loose. They had searched the fair from top to bottom. Twinkle Toes was strutting around Blanche's feet when they trudged back into the poultry barn.

"What did you do to my bird?" sputtered Grandpa when he spotted Blanche.

"I didn't touch your crazy chicken," said Blanche. "She bit through the zip tie and busted out of that flimsy cage all on her own. She must be running around the fairgrounds."

"We looked everywhere," said Grandpa.

Twinkle Toes tried to jump up to the table and fell

back. "You need a little boost," said Blanche, picking up her chicken.

"A little boost," repeated Charlie. He had heard Blanche say those words before. His eyes widened and he raced toward the door.

"Where are you going?" asked Grandma.

"All's fair in love and chicken racing," shouted Charlie.

"What does that mean?" yelled Grandpa.

"It means I know where the dragon is," answered Charlie. He hurried to the parking lot and ran down the row of cars and trucks until he found Blanche's Ford.

Charlie looked in the back of the truck but the dragon wasn't there. He was turning to leave when he heard a clucking sound coming from inside the cab.

Charlie opened the door and the dragon came

shooting out. She blasted across the parking lot with Charlie hot on her tail. She headed straight for the baked goods building and ran through the front door.

There was a wild commotion as Charlie and the dragon hurtled into the building. People crashed into each other trying to get out of the way of Charlie and the huge chicken.

Charlie slammed into a table full of fruit pies. The table flipped, sending the pies into the air like fruit-filled flying saucers. Charlie fell into the pile of pies before getting to his feet and charging after the dragon.

Grandpa's crazy chicken jumped onto a table full of cakes and high-stepped it from cake to cake. Charlie made a wild grab and ended up with a faceful of frosting as the dragon leapfrogged a coconut layer cake and landed smack dab in the middle of a Texas Sheet Cake.

Charlie wiped the frosting from his eyes just in time to see the dragon jump onto the next table. She galloped through the cream pies like a moose in a snowstorm. With a flying leap Charlie belly flopped onto the table. He grabbed the dragon's left leg just as she was about to plunge into a lemon meringue pie.

"I caught you," shouted Charlie.

"And I caught you," said a policeman as he grabbed the back of Charlie's shirt.

Officer Bowen marched Charlie over to a chair in the corner of the building. Charlie sat down and the officer took out a small notebook.

"You two have made quite a mess," said Officer Bowen. "What's your name?"

Charlie took a deep breath and began to spill his guts. "I'm Charlie Bacon and this is the dragon. She's not really a dragon. She's a chicken. She's my grandpa's chicken. She's crazy. She tried to kill my grandma but ended up biting Grandpa's behind instead. Then Mrs. Trudeau chicken-napped her. Grandma went to get the dragon back and that's when she bought Zippy."

"Who's Zippy?" asked Officer Bowen as he tried to scribble down everything Charlie was saying.

"Zippy's a chicken but she's not the top of the pecking order because Grandpa is the big chicken," said Charlie.

"Grandpa is a chicken?" asked the officer. "I thought you were talking about your grandfather."

"I am," said Charlie. "Grandma says he's the biggest chicken. He rides bucking bulls too. He could have gone professional but decided to unplug toilets instead."

Officer Bowen scratched his head and asked, "What does any of this have to do with ruining all of these cakes and pies? There's something you're not telling me."

"Cluck Cluck," blurted Charlie.

"Cluck Cluck?" said the officer who was looking more confused by the second. "Son, I think maybe you've hit your head and need to see a doctor."

"Cluck Cluck is the chicken I'm racing in the Super Cooper," said Charlie.

"Is this somehow tied to the chicken race this afternoon?" asked Officer Bowen.

"Yes," said Charlie. "Mrs. Trudeau let the dragon out of her cage because she's afraid that the dragon will beat Twinkle Toes in the race. But Cluck Cluck is going to beat them both because she has a secret ingredient."

Charlie looked up when he heard someone call his name. It was Grandma and she was staring at her prize-winning pie that was smashed on the floor. She picked up the broken pie plate and marched over to Charlie and Officer Bowen.

"I'm Charlie's grandmother. Is he being arrested?" she asked.

"No one is being arrested, at least not yet," said Officer Bowen. "I need to do some investigating first. Charlie's story is very confusing but I think someone else is responsible for this chicken being loose."

"I think I can clear things up a bit," said Grandma.

"Can I leave?" asked Charlie. "The race is about to begin."

"You can go," said Officer Bowen. "Tell Cluck Cluck good luck for me."

"She doesn't need luck, she has a secret ingredient," said Charlie. He tucked the dragon under his arm football-style and raced out the door.

Chapter 11

The Big Race

Charlie found a water hose and cleaned up the best he could before sprinting into the poultry barn. "I caught the dragon!" he shouted when he spotted Grandpa. "Can we still make it to the race?"

"The racers have already been called to the track," said Grandpa, taking the dragon from Charlie. "We've got to hurry."

"But I need to get some strawberries. They're Cluck Cluck's secret ingredient," said Charlie.

"There's no time," said Grandpa.

The other racers were already at the Super Cooper racetrack when Charlie and Grandpa arrived. The track was a huge oval track with individual starting gates for the chickens.

Cluck Cluck was assigned starting gate nine. She was between a colorful chicken named Fireball and a speckled orange hen named Mary. The dragon was in gate three and Twinkle Toes was two gates over in gate five.

"Racers, load your chickens," boomed the announcer's voice.

"Run like the wind," said Charlie as he placed Cluck Cluck in the starting gate. He then followed the other handlers around the track so they could cheer their birds on down the homestretch. Charlie found a large feeding bucket to stand on so he could have a bird's-eye view of the track.

A tall, skinny man fired the starter's pistol in the air and all the gates popped open at once. The crowd went wild as the chickens sprinted onto the track. The

dragon blasted to the front of the pack like a runaway train.

"That's my girl," yelled Grandpa.

Twinkle Toes soon caught her and they were running neck and neck. Cluck Cluck was at the back of the pack next to Fireball. As the chickens headed for the first turn, Blanche stuck her whistle in her mouth and let out a loud blast. The shrill sound seemed to energize Twinkle Toes. She lowered her head and quickly took the lead.

Twinkle Toes and the dragon were running at top speed as they came to the second turn.

"Slow down or you won't make the turn," yelled Grandpa.

The dragon didn't slow down and hit the fence at full speed. She ran straight up the wire and out of the racetrack.

"You dumb bird!" yelled Grandpa as he chased after the dragon into the fairgrounds.

That left Twinkle Toes all by herself at the front of the pack. She extended her lead with every stride. The crowd was cheering and stomping as the chickens headed into the homestretch.

That's when Cluck Cluck looked up and saw her secret ingredient. She loved strawberries. But she loved Charlie Bacon more. Her eyes narrowed as she charged down the track toward her best friend.

Cluck Cluck blasted past Fireball and left Mary in her dust. She passed seven other chickens before moving close to Twinkle Toes' tail feathers. She made a move to pass Twinkle Toes on the right but Twinkle Toes cut her off.

Cluck Cluck then tried to pass on the left but Twinkle Toes bumped into her and she almost went down. Charlie held his breath as Cluck Cluck regained her footing and quickly caught back up.

With five feet to go Cluck Cluck leaped in the air. It seemed like everything went into slow motion as she gracefully sailed over the top of Twinkle Toes. Cluck Cluck landed right in stride and sprinted across the finish line.

"And the winner is Cluck Cluck!" declared the announcer.

Charlie couldn't believe it. "She won! She won! She won!" he repeated as he hurried onto the track to pick up his champion.

The crowd was still cheering when Grandma finally arrived. "We won!" whooped Charlie.

Grandma gave Charlie a huge hug and then looked around for Grandpa. "Where's your grandfather?" she asked.

"The dragon jumped the track and ran off. Grandpa chased after her," explained Charlie.

"Oh dear," said Grandma. "We better help him."

"First, I have to collect my winnings," said Charlie. He carried Cluck Cluck to the winner's podium. The Locket County Cheese Princess presented him with the Super Cooper trophy and a check for two hundred dollars.

"What are you going to do with all that money?" asked the announcer.

"I'm getting my grandpa a new cowboy hat and my grandma a new pie plate. With the rest I'm buying fried pickles," answered Charlie.

"That's a lot of pickles," said the announcer.

"I'm a lot of boy," said Charlie, grinning.

Charlie looked into the crowd and spotted Officer Bowen standing next to the short, stocky man from the poultry barn. When the man pointed out Blanche Trudeau, Officer Bowen made a beeline in her direction.

Blanche tried to make a getaway but Officer Bowen was too quick. Charlie knew that Blanche Trudeau's cheating ways had finally caught up to her.

Just then the dragon burst out of the crowd with Grandpa hot on its trail. The wild bird headed straight for Grandma.

"Catch that dragon!" yelled Grandpa.

Before Charlie could move, Grandma grabbed the large feeding bucket and slammed it over the top of the chicken just as it got to her. She quickly sat on the bucket and folded her arms in victory. The crowd cheered loudly for the fantastic dragon catcher.

About the Author

Gary Hogg is the author of more than twenty books. His hilarious stories include *Look What the Cat Dragged In*, *I Heard of a Nerd Bird*, and the popular *Spencer's Adventures* series. Gary says his fourth grade teacher inspired him to put his wild ideas into stories instead of acting them out in class. She kept her sanity and he became a writer. Of all the characters he's created, Gary says Charlie Bacon is the most like him.

Gary is a popular speaker and guest author. He has inspired over 2 million students to be better writers with his popular *Writing is Exciting!* assembly and workshop program. You can learn about him at **www.garyhoggbooks.com**.